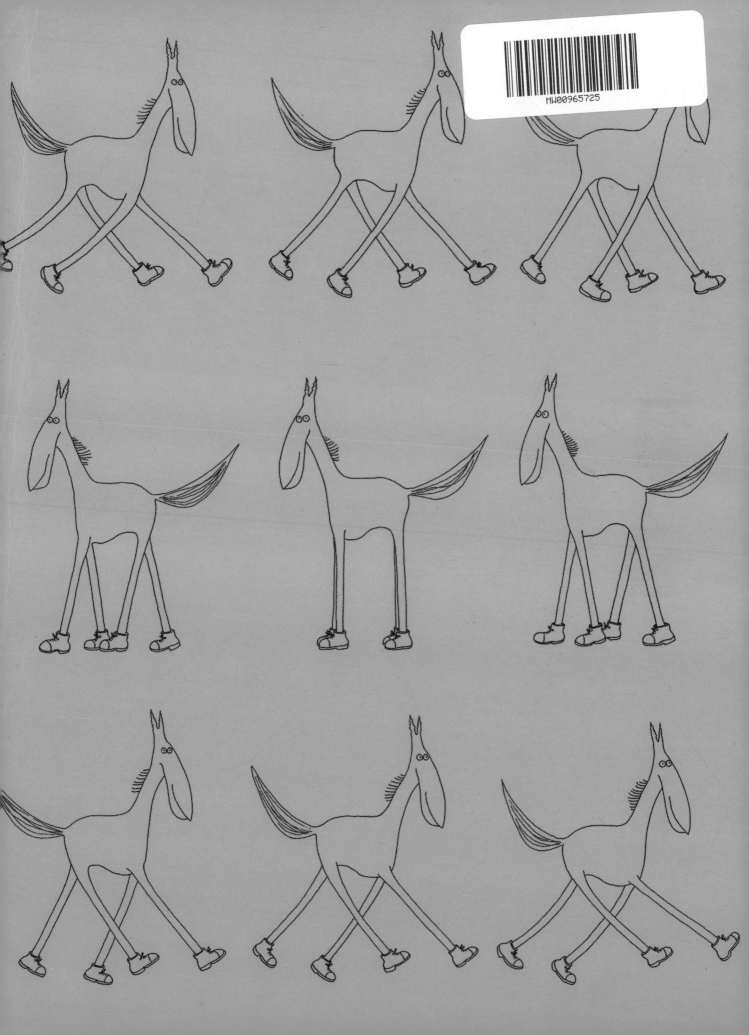

Horsy-hops

A Newfoundland Bestiary

Breakwater Books
100 Water Street
P.O. Box 2188
St. John's, NL
A1C 6E6

National Library of Canada Cataloguing in Publication

Barton, Anthony, 1942-
Horsy-hops / Anthony Barton.

ISBN 1-55081-200-9

1. Folklore--Newfoundland and Labrador--Juvenile poetry.
2. Newfoundland and Labrador--Social life and customs--Juvenile poetry.
3. Children's poetry, Canadian (English)
        I. Title.

PS8553.A7776H67 2003   jC811'.6   C2003-903330-9

Design & Layout: Carola Kern, Rhonda Molloy
Cover Design: Rhonda Molloy

The Canada Council | Le Conseil des Arts
for the Arts | du Canada

We acknowledge the financial support of The Canada Council for the Arts for our publishing activities.

Canada   We acknowledge the financial support of the Government of Canada through the Book Publishing Industry Development Program (BPIDP) for our publishing activities.

Printed in Canada

Horsy-hops

A Newfoundland Bestiary

Story & Pictures by Anthony Barton

For Sophia and Farah

If you are bad and put your moose
into your mother's orange juice,
she'll telephone the Horsy-hops,
the Horsy-hops, the Horsy-hops,
the terrible awful Horsy-hops
to carry you away.

If Horsy-hops can't come today,
she'll send for others of his gang:
old Boobagger and Owenshook
and Beachy Bird and Angle-dog
and dreadful frightful Bullymaroo
and then what will you do?

Horsy-hops's boots

WONK
WONK
WONK
WONK
WONK

Horsy-hops

The Horsy-hops is six foot two.
I'd watch for him if I were you.
His mane is green his legs are blue
and...
WONK WONK WONK WONK
go his rubber boots.

WONK

WONK

WONK

WONK

If I were you I'd not despair
when he rears up and paws the air—
I'd ask him where he's taking you
with a...
WONK WONK WONK WONK
of his rubber boots.

The Horsy-hops is not so bright.
Your query will give him a fright.
He'll stop to think and you'll have time
to...
WONK WONK WONK WONK
steal his rubber boots.

While Horsy-hops is standing there
wondering why his feet are bare,
you can go clumping home and drink
tea...
from his rubber boots.

Horsy-hops [n] a horse which carries off humans. If you meet a horsy-hops, put your hands
over your eyes and say WONK WONK.

Boobagger

The Boobagger's cry is a dreadful BOO!
He leaps out of hiding to startle you.

Shout BOO TO YOU and yell TIT FOR TAT
and snatch off his beautiful toadstool hat!

He wants his hat back for his head is bare
and that poor old Boobagger has no hair.

So give back his hat and be mild and meek
and ask him to join you for Hide and Seek.

Boobagger [n] a little man who lives under your house. If you are surprised by a boobagger, put your hands over your ears and say BOO TO YOU and TIT FOR TAT.

Boo Man's hat [n] a Newfoundland toadstool.

Owenshook

The Owenshook's a copy cat,
he copies what you do.

So when you play at Tiddly Sticks
he likes to tiddly too.

Although he's really not so bad,
his constant games may drive you mad!

So play a game of nursery
and he will let you be.

Owenshook [n] a fool. If an owenshook bothers you, say NURR-MURR.

Tiddly [n] a game played with sticks and stones. Find a short stick, a long stick and a small beach rock. Place the short stick leaning against the beach rock. Use the long stick to hook the short stick up into the air. See how far you can make the short stick fly. If another player catches your short stick while it is flying through the air, it is his or her turn. If you flip your short stick the furthest, you win.

Beachy Bird

The Beachy Bird is fond of treats.
He runs along the shore.
He dashes to the waves and eats
then dashes back for more.

So if you want to pet this bird
I'll tell you what to do:

Pretend you run a restaurant.
Invite him out to dine.

Feed him all the treats he wants
and you'll get along just fine!

Beachy Bird [n] a sandpiper. If you meet a beachy bird, put some seaweed on your head and WHISTLE.

Angle-dog

The Angle-dog's a horrid beast,
the ugliest from west to east.

Tell Angle-dog to splash about
and up will pop a handsome trout

and both of you can watch that trout
to see just how he swims about.

Then kiss the dog and you will see
him gently let that trout go free.

Angle-dog [n] a worm used for trouting. If you meet an angle-dog, say SWISHY FISHY.

Bullymaroo

And last and worst is Bullymaroo,
the horrible frightful Bullymaroo!

He's here: the awful Bullymaroo.
You'd better say "How d'you doodly-doo?"

"So pleased to meet you, Bullymaroo,
and here's a little gift for you."

And when you go he'll never know
for you'll depart on tippy-toe.

Bullymaroo [n] an aggressive bully. If you have no ribbon to give him, turn your coat inside out
and shout HUNKY PUNKY.

Now you've outwitted every beast!
It's time to have your birthday feast.
You know who you'll invite to come
so write and ask them one by one:
the Horsy-hops, the Horsy-hops,
the terrible awful Horsy-hops,
old Boobagger and Owenshook
and Beachy Bird and Angle-dog
and horrible frightful Bullymaroo—
he'll have to be invited too.

And when they come you'll have a time:
you'll sing and dance and play and mime

and when you want to have some fun
you'll show your beasts how turtles run.

Turtles [n] a party game. Snip your own turtles out of cardboard boxes. Make each turtle 16 inches high. Use a pencil to make a hole for the string. Place the hole 7 inches from the tip of the turtle's nose. Thread the string through the hole. If you do not have a horsy-hops, tie the strings to the legs of a chair instead. Players must stay behind the starting line. Make your turtle run by wiggling the string. See whose turtle wins.

And now they have their backs to you.
I wonder: Do you know who's who?

WONK   WONK   WONK   WONK

The Horsy-hops Song

Words: Anthony Barton
Music: Fergus O'Byrne

Lively

The Horsy-hops Song

adapted by Fergus O'Byrne

(Verses 1 and 2 are sung to the first page of the music.)

1. If you are bad and put your moose
   into your mother's orange juice,
   she'll telephone the Horsy-hops,
   the Horsy-hops, the Horsy-hops,
   the terrible awful Horsy-hops
   to carry you away.

2. If Horsy-hops can't come today,
   she'll make these others come your way:
   old Boobagger and Owenshook
   and Beachy Bird and Angle-dog
   and dreadful frightful Bullymaroo
   and then what will you do?

(Verses 3 to 10 are sung to the second page of the music.)

3. The Horsy-hops is six foot two.
   I'd watch for him if I were you.
   His mane is green, his legs are blue
   and WONK WONK WONK WONK
   go his rubber boots.

   When he rears up and paws the air
   if I were you I'd not despair.
   When he takes you just ask him where
   with a WONK WONK WONK WONK
   of his rubber boots.

4. The Horsy-hops is not so bright.
   You'll baffle him all through the night.
   He'll stop and you will be all right
   to WONK WONK WONK WONK
   steal his rubber boots.

   While Horsy-hops is standing there
   wondering why his feet are bare,
   go clumping home and tea prepare
   and WONK WONK WONK WONK
   in his rubber boots.

5. The Boobagger gives a big BOO!
   He leaps right out to startle you.
   Yell TIT FOR TAT, shout BOO TO YOU
   and BOO HOO HOO HOO
   grab his toadstool hat!

   He wants his hat, his head is bare.
   Poor old Boobagger has no hair.
   Be mild and meek and kind and fair
   and BOO HOO HOO HOO
   play some Hide and Seek.

6. The Owenshook's a copy cat,
   he always copies what you're at.
   Play Tiddly Sticks and he'll do that
   and HOOK HOOK HOOK HOOK
   play at Tiddly too.

   Although he's really not so bad,
   his constant games may drive you mad!
   Play nursery so he'll be glad
   to HOOK HOOK HOOK HOOK
   and he will let you be.

7. The Beachy Bird is fond of treats.
   He darts along on twinkling feet.
   He dashes to the waves and eats
   with a CHOMP CHOMP CHOMP CHOMP
   then goes back for more.

   Now if this bird you want to pet
   invite him out to dine a bit.
   Feed him treats and I will bet
   he'll CHOMP CHOMP CHOMP CHOMP
   you'll get along just fine!

8. The Angle-dog's a horrid beast,
   the ugliest from west to east.
   If Angle-dog will splash at least
   with a SWISH SWISH SWISH SWISH
   you will catch a trout.

   And both of you can watch that trout
   to see just how he swims about.
   But kiss the dog, without a doubt
   with a SWISH SWISH SWISH SWISH
   he lets the trout go free.

9. And last and worst is Bullymaroo,
   the horrible old Bullymaroo!
   He's here: the awful Bullymaroo,
   with a WOO WOO WOO WOO
   how d'you doodly-doo?

   "So pleased to meet you, Bullymaroo,
   and here's a little gift for you."
   And when you go what will you do?
   With a WOO WOO WOO WOO
   you'll go on tippy-toe.

10. Now you've outwitted every beast!
    From north and south and west and east.
    It's time to have your birthday feast
    and CLAP CLAP CLAP CLAP
    ask them one by one.

    And when they come you'll have a time.
    The beasts will join us in our rhyme.
    We'll sing and dance and play and mime
    and CLAP CLAP CLAP CLAP
    dance with everyone:

    (Verse 11 is sung to the first page of the music.)

11. The Horsy-hops, the Horsy-hops,
    the terrible awful Horsy-hops,
    old Boobagger and Owenshook
    and Beachy Bird and Angle-dog
    and dreadful frightful Bullymaroo.
    They're all friends with you!

About the author:

Anthony Barton is a painter and writer who has lived in Newfoundland for twenty-eight years. He has had two sell-out exhibitions of his paintings in St. John's, both funded by the Newfoundland and Labrador Council for the Arts. His work has been published by Methuen, Simon & Schuster and Penguin.

About the musician:

Fergus O'Byrne, originally from Ireland, is a well known musician who has won several music awards. He has performed extensively on radio and television both in Canada and abroad, and continues to tour nationally and internationally. Fergus has developed a curriculum-based school production, which he presents throughout Newfoundland and Labrador. Both his television and sound recordings also contribute to various levels of school and university programming in the province and he has been involved in several ArtsSmarts projects.

About the horsy-hops:

Horsy-hops's boot size is number 12. He has lived in Newfoundland all his life. He was born in the Crow's Hole at Job's Cove. His hobbies are collecting beach rocks and t'ai chi. He loves to sing and dance.